The Zero Hour

by Madeleine George

A SAMUEL FRENCH ACTING EDITION

SAMUEL FRENCH

FOUNDED 1830

NEW YORK HOLLYWOOD LONDON TORONTO

SAMUELFRENCH.COM

ISBN 978-0-573-69920-7   Printed in U.S.A.   #29862

MUSIC USE NOTE

Licensees are solely responsible for obtaining formal written permission from copyright owners to use copyrighted music in the performance of this play and are strongly cautioned to do so. If no such permission is obtained by the licensee, then the licensee must use only original music that the licensee owns and controls. Licensees are solely responsible and liable for all music clearances and shall indemnify the copyright owners of the play and their licensing agent, Samuel French, Inc., against any costs, expenses, losses and liabilities arising from the use of music by licensees.

IMPORTANT BILLING AND CREDIT
REQUIREMENTS

All producers of *THE ZERO HOUR must* give credit to the Author of the Play in all programs distributed in connection with performances of the Play, and in all instances in which the title of the Play appears for the purposes of advertising, publicizing or otherwise exploiting the Play and/or a production. The name of the Author *must* appear on a separate line on which no other name appears, immediately following the title and *must* appear in size of type not less than fifty percent of the size of the title type.

THE ZERO HOUR was first produced by 13P at Walkerspace in New York City on June 22, 2010. The performance was directed by Adam Greenfield and produced by Rachel Karpf (Preston Copley, associate producer), with sets by Mimi Lien, costumes by Sydney Maresca, lighting by Ben Kato, and sound by Asa Wember. The production stage manager was Sunneva Stapleton. The cast was as follows:

O . . . . Hannah Cabell

REBECCA . . . . Angela Goethals

THE ALL-AMERICAN NAZI, AKA "DOUG" . . . . Gardiner Comfort

CHARACTERS

O – 26, butch dyke, intense, unemployed, recovering WASP

THE THERAPIST – 45

THE LONELY NAZI

THE EAGER NAZI

THE TENDER NAZI

> …all played by the actor who plays O

REBECCA – 29, corporate femme, educated, graceful, Jewish

RAE WILCOX – 59, **O**'s mother

LILY HIRSCHORN – 64, **REBECCA**'s mother

> …both played by the actor who plays **REBECCA**

THE ALL-AMERICAN NAZI, a.k.a. "DOUG," 32

SETTING

Queens, New York

TIME

January and February

AUTHOR'S NOTES

Sets should be minimal, suggestive of the urban spaces – both indoor and outdoor – that the play takes place in. The bedroom of O and Rebecca's apartment is always present onstage, and its borders are permeable; subway cars and therapists' offices and sports bars move fluidly in and out of its space.

Costume changes are part of the action and should be made by the actors themselves onstage during scene shifts, in view of the audience. Perhaps the actors even help each other dress and undress. Costumes may be stored in the closets or drawers of the bedroom set for this purpose.

History is the subject of a structure whose site is not homogeneous, empty time, but time filled with the presence of the now.

Walter Benjamin, Thesis XIV,
"Theses on the Philosophy of History"

Scene One

(The bedroom of a scummy sixth-floor walk-up, next to the elevated subway track.)

(No walls – black night and the lights of the low Queens skyline on all sides.)

(An oily, orange three-quarter moon hangs huge on the horizon.)

(O and REBECCA curled into each other. REBECCA asleep. A subway train approaches.)

(O wakes.)

O. *(quiet, thoughtful)* I think my mother may just have died.

(The subway train grows louder, explodes past the bedroom window. REBECCA stirs, resettles on O's chest.)

(quiet, mildly surprised) I think my mother may be about to die.

REBECCA. *(asleep)* Mmmm?

O. Shhhhh…

(O strokes REBECCA's head. Lights shift.)

Scene Two

(The kitchenette. O *and* REBECCA. *The onset of dinner.*
O *with a Polaroid camera)*

O. Let me see you with the tuna fish. Hold up the can.

*(*REBECCA *poses ridiculously with a fork and an empty
tuna can.* O *takes her picture – flash!)*

"Rebecca Eats Tuna." Get it? Get it?

REBECCA. I get it. What is it with you and the snapshots?

O. Nothing. I'm just saving you up for later.

(In one motion, O *kisses* REBECCA, *stows the camera
and photo away, and sits down. They start to eat.)*

So how'd it go with Hitler today?

REBECCA. Great for him. Not so great for us. He's busy
rising to power right now.

O. You're doing the before part, too?

REBECCA. Three parts: "The Growing Storm": Versailles,
Beer Hall Putsch, death of Hindenburg, et cetera. Part
Two: "Into the Night," that's the blood and gore. Then
"Lessons for the Living." They want me to end it very
Hands-Across-America: "Six million Jews died during
the Holocaust so be nice and don't call each other
Spic and Kike."

O. And Fag. And Dyke.

REBECCA. That's right.

*(*REBECCA *chews.)*

O. Are you gonna say that, though?

REBECCA. Fag and Dyke? I don't know.

O. You should.

REBECCA. I guess. It's seventh grade.

O. So? If they can see pictures of bodies being bulldozed
into open graves they can see the word 'homosexual'
on a page, I should think.

REBECCA. *(totally noncommittal)* I should think so.

(O *considers* **REBECCA** *critically.*)

O. You're not going to put anything about all the gay guys that died in there, are you? You know, that's where the pink triangle *comes* from.

REBECCA. *(weary)* I know, I know…

O. That sucks. Spookie? I think that sucks.

REBECCA. They want to sell it to schools all over the country. If you even *mention* sexuality half these Bible Belt districts go completely apeshit. It's just demographics.

O. You think it's okay for kids to learn some warped version of the truth just because Chicken Little Pamphleteers and Propagandists wants to sell more books to the Christian Right?

REBECCA. *(irritated)* It's Mother Goose Educational Texts.

O. Do they know you're dating me?

REBECCA. What does that have –

O. *(overlapping)* Do they know that you're living with a woman at work?

REBECCA. *(attempt at levity #1)* I'm not living with a woman at work.

(O *squints at* **REBECCA** *unforgivingly.* **REBECCA** *rolls her eyes.*)

So what?

O. But they know you're Jewish, right?

REBECCA. So?

O. *(triumphant)* So, so, so!

REBECCA. *What?*

O. It just seems all very, all very convenient. All very dishonest.

REBECCA. We're a children's educational publishing house, O. It's irrelevant to the way I do my job. It's none of anybody else's business.

O. I'm out all the time. Out of respect for you.

REBECCA. You don't have a *job*! *Where* are you out? You're out when you go to unem*ploy*ment?

O. I'm out every second of every day. I'm out at the Key Food. I'm out at the bodega.

REBECCA. You're not out at the bodega. I've seen you flirt with that guy for extra matches.

O. I'm out to my hygienist at Praise the Lord Dental.

REBECCA. *(attempt at levity #2)* Well, you're very fierce. I'm sure you'll get into Lesbian Heaven and I'll spend eternity trapped in some overheated room with 25 other closet cases, talking about our need to please our mothers.

O. *(a shade vicious)* Serve you right if you did.

*(***REBECCA*** *pulls back.)*

REBECCA. You're hard, you know, O.

(They pick at their plates for a second, listlessly.)

O. *(quiet)* Speaking of mothers...

REBECCA. Tomorrow at one. El Azteco on 53rd.

O. I assume you don't want me to...

REBECCA. Maybe next time.

(Lights shift.)

Scene Three

*(**REBECCA** downstage in writing light. She works on her textbook.)*

REBECCA. *(evenly)* Building Your Vocabulary. Using construction paper, magic markers and brads, make a glossary of important Holocaust terms. Organize your glossary alphabetically, and begin with the basics. Allies. Anti-Semitism. Aryan. Atrocity. As you learn more about this period of history, add terms that are unfamiliar to you to your glossary. Illustrate your glossary with colorful pictures cut from magazines to help you remember what the new terms mean.

(Lights shift.)

Scene Four

(**REBECCA** *in session, down left of the bedroom, slumped deep in an armchair as if she's been flung there.* **THE THERAPIST** *sits opposite, her head balanced lightly on the tips of her fingers.* **THE THERAPIST** *is lushly feminine in a practical way – gentle fabrics, wooden jewelry, clogs of some kind. She looks at* **REBECCA** *calmly, consumingly.* **REBECCA** *froths.*)

REBECCA. I love her, but I'm not gay.

THE THERAPIST. Okay.

REBECCA. I love sleeping with her, but I'm not gay.

THE THERAPIST. Okay.

REBECCA. Which means I must not love her or love sleeping with her in the way I'm supposed to. Love her or love sleeping with her. If I'm not gay. This bores you.

THE THERAPIST. No.

REBECCA. I'm sorry.

THE THERAPIST. I'm not bored. And we're not here for me. Can I ask you: What does it mean to be "gay"?

REBECCA. Well. It means. That you're, you know, a homo – lesbian.

THE THERAPIST. A homolesbian?

REBECCA. It means, it's about identity, not behavior.

THE THERAPIST. (*nodding, about to challenge her*) So –

REBECCA. Can we talk about Nazis? Please?

(*beat*)

THE THERAPIST. We can talk about anything you want to talk about.

REBECCA. Good, because Nazis have been on my mind a lot lately.

THE THERAPIST. What about Nazis do you want to talk about?

REBECCA. Well, their cruelty.

THE THERAPIST. Okay.

REBECCA. Also their false transcendental ahistoricism.

(beat)

THE THERAPIST. All right.

REBECCA. By which I mean the way they seem to embody an absolute standard of evil for so many people in America. That really bothers me, you know, the idea that Nazis are the be-all and end-all of worldly evil, because it takes a lot of other really evil people off the hook, that idea.

THE THERAPIST. So you'd like to put Nazi war crimes into a kind of perspective.

REBECCA. Why not? I mean, yes. I don't see why we should have to tiptoe around this event, this admittedly completely horrifying, time-shattering event –

THE THERAPIST. You're referring to the Holocaust itself –

REBECCA. – I'm referring to the Holocaust itself – why we have to put this event up on a pedestal and tiptoe around it like it's somehow sanctified, like it's peerless in its horror, when there are plenty of genocides around that are just as horrible. There are dozens of genocides I can think of just off the top of my head.

(to herself)

Name one.

*(to **THE THERAPIST***)*

Okay: The slaughter of the Armenians by the Turks. Stalin's liquidization of the kulaks. Pol Pot. The Massacre at Wounded Knee, for an example that hits a little closer to home. I mean, who's to say which of these events was the most blood-soaked, the most affronting to Enlightenment principles, and why do we feel compelled to compare them in the first place? Why does there have to be a gold medal winner in the Who-Committed-the-Worst-Crime-Against-Humanity Competition? Surely for each individual starved or macheted or bayoneted through the back of the head their own death was the most memorable, the most tragic, the most illustrative of man's inhumanity to man, et cetera?

THE THERAPIST. What I'm hearing is that you're thinking a lot about atrocities lately.

REBECCA. Yes. No. I'm thinking about honesty. I'm thinking a lot about honesty lately.

(Lights shift.)

Scene Five

(Nighttime. The apartment, the bedroom. Rainstorm outside. We hear the hiss of the downpour, occasional thunder. No moon tonight – cloudcover.)

(O is on the bed reading Martha Stewart Living. *The bedroom is filled with a wide assortment of vessels – pans, plates, buckets, tupperware containers, empty milk cartons – set out all over the floor, dresser, bed, etc. to catch the drips that are pouring from the ceiling. Real water isn't necessary – the musical sound of a roomful of plopping, splashing drips is enough.)*

*(**REBECCA** appears in the bathroom doorway in a terry-cloth robe, toweling off her wet hair.)*

REBECCA. *(re: showering)* Why did I even bother?

O. It's the price you pay for living in the penthouse.

REBECCA. Don't we have a super or somebody we could call about this? I mean, this is ridiculous.

O. People who live in apartments with supers who have phones pay a lot more rent than we do.

REBECCA. Well, I believe I can see the value of that equation.

(She maps it out for O in the air.)

Pay guy rent. Have guy come and fix holes in ceiling through which water pours and drenches bed. Bed now dry, as a direct result of paying guy rent. Everybody happy. Capitalism at its cleanest and most straightforward.

O. It's funny that you should mention capitalism, because I've been thinking –

REBECCA. *(hopefully)* About getting a job?

O. *(surprised)* No.

(grossed out)

No.

REBECCA. Oh.

O. What is it, exactly, that upsets you so much about me not having a job?

REBECCA. It doesn't *upset* me...

O. You mention it constantly.

REBECCA. I just wonder, I mean, don't you get bored?

O. Never. I have a jam-packed schedule.

REBECCA. Really. What's on it?

O. Well, let's see. Today I read an article from last week's Arts and Leisure about the Theater of Cruelty and its impact on the Broadway musical.

(She indicates her copy of Martha Stewart Living.*)*

Then I consulted with a home repair expert about how to create faux painted wood paneling – I'm thinking of doing the walls over, maybe.

REBECCA. *(raised eyebrows, feigned interest)* Oh.

O. And then I rode the 7 from Flushing to Times Square and back for a while.

REBECCA. Like, without getting off?

O. Of course. I ride the 7 a lot.

REBECCA. Um, why?

O. *(this is obvious)* Because it's beautiful.

REBECCA. The 7 train?

O. You take it every day. Don't you find it beautiful?

REBECCA. Not really. I mean, it's a commute...

O. Are you kidding? Don't you know how lucky you are that you fell in love with a girl who lives on an el? What if I lived in like, Yorkville or something, and you had to crawl into some hole in the ground and shove your way onto the *4* every morning? Do you know how demoralizing that would be?

REBECCA. I've taken the 4, it's not that bad.

O. *(incredulous)* Are you *kidding*? Compared to the *7*?

REBECCA. You know, I'm a fairly experienced rider of New York public transit. Although I don't know if I would do it – recreationally...

O. *(rhapsodic)* The rooftops of Queens stretching out in a hazy landscape like the atmosphere of a golden planet all the way to the Manhattan skyline, which comes closer and closer like an event horizon as you crest the wave of Long Island City…

REBECCA. I guess it's a nice way to kill a few hours.

(beat)

O. That's right, riding the 7 is killing time. Standing around the Xerox talking about who's got the wittiest New Yorker cartoon in their cube, that's *work*.

REBECCA. Excuse me?

O. No, I know it's pretty staggeringly important stuff, deciding which castrated version of history to cram down the throats of America's youth.

REBECCA. You know, this whole noble savage act is all very attractive, but I'd be careful if I were you.

O. Oh, I'm sorry, am I offending the breadwinner?

REBECCA. *(serious)* Yes, you are.

*(**REBECCA** exits back into the bathroom. A beat. **O** slumps.)*

O. *(half to herself)* Okay, that sucked.

(Beat. Calling off)

Spookie, I'm sorry. I shouldn't have said that. It sucked.

(beat)

I know you work hard.

REBECCA. *(from off, aggrieved)* I do.

O. I know. I appreciate how hard you work.

(beat)

That was horrible, what I just said. I'm sorry. Come back.

*(**REBECCA** appears in the doorway, minus towel. She folds her arms over her chest.)*

REBECCA. *(stretching it out)* I don't know. I don't know how I feel about you right now.

O. Please, Spookie, I was just being stupid.

REBECCA. You are stupid.

O. I am. I'm a savage. Housebreak me.

> *(O makes a space next to her in a nest of pillows.*
> **REBECCA** *climbs gingerly onto the bed, avoiding the*
> *sloshing buckets. She snuggles up against* **O.***)*

REBECCA. My mother called me three times at work today.

> *(O sighs.)*

O. And?

REBECCA. She wants to know when I'm going to get a land-line in my new place. She says she doesn't understand why it's taking them so long to install it. She said if I don't get a landline installed within the next three days she's going to send me a cell phone so she can reach me when I'm not at work.

O. It's insane that you don't have a cell phone.

> *(REBECCA shrugs.)*

REBECCA. I don't always like to be reached.

O. Why don't you just *give* her this number?

REBECCA. Because what if you pick up and it's her?

O. Tell her you have a roommate. Isn't that standard evasive procedure in these situations?

REBECCA. It's hard for me to lie to her.

O. *(sarcasm)* Yeah, I can see that.

REBECCA. I just mean, the more complicated I make my lie, the harder it is for me to pull it off.

> *(beat)*

You're so lucky you and your mother don't speak.

> *(beat)*

I told her to go ahead and send me the cell.

> *(Lights shift.)*

Scene Six

*(**REBECCA** downstage in writing light. She works on her textbook.)*

REBECCA. *(evenly)* Debating Controversial Issues. With your classmates, form two opposing teams. Have each team argue for one resolution to the following dilemma. A young Jewish woman, living in Berlin in 1938, has the opportunity to obtain a set of documents that falsely identify her as being of Aryan descent. Kristallnacht has recently taken place and all the young woman's Jewish friends are trying to emigrate, but the young woman loves her job, she loves Berlin. It is the only life she has ever known. Should she procure the false documents, enabling herself to stay where she is but dooming herself to live in constant fear of exposure? Or should she reveal her true identity, and sacrifice her entire life as she knows it?

(beat)

Defend your position.

(Lights shift.)

Scene Seven

(The bedroom, dusty 10:00 a.m. light. O, in A-shirt and boxers, preparing to get dressed. RAE, dressed as for church – sedate suit, purse, reasonable pumps – sitting primly on the edge of the unmade bed. RAE is an elegant 59, a lifelong tennis player.)

(As they talk, O assesses three identical shirts, selects one, puts it on.)

RAE. Well, this room is nice. Did you do the ceiling special?

O. If you're referring to the water stains, they were here when I moved in.

RAE. I was not referring to the water stains. I was trying to compliment you.

O. See, this is why I would never have let you come here in real life. I could have seen that you would go right for the stains.

RAE. I'm saying it looks nice! It's clear you've put some thought into the place.

O. And muscle.

RAE. Well it shows. I can only imagine what it looked like when you moved in.

(O pulls on very butch pants, jingling with keys, belt, change – boy stuff.)

Now this, however, upsets me.

(O sighs, turns her back on her mother.)

No, I'm going to speak about this. I'll never understand why you – you have such a lovely –

O. *(desperately)* Mother –

RAE. No, it's not embarrassing. It shouldn't shame you for me to discuss the facts. You have a very lovely, perfectly *womanly* body –

O. For the love of Pete –

RAE. – and I'll never understand why you feel compelled
to board it up like an abandoned building in those, in
those I-can-hardly-call-them-clothes. You say you're not
a success as a heterosexual but darling, I think those
slacks may have something to do with it.

O. It's a – you've got the chicken and egg mixed up.

RAE. I have no idea what you mean. Is that some kind of
homosexual code?

O. No, it's –

RAE. Speak to me as if I were a sexless old woman.

O. *(mapping it out in the air: body under, clothes over)* I'm the
queer. I buy the pants to match.

(**RAE** *makes a face.*)

RAE. I don't know why you have to talk like that.

(**O** *shrugs.*)

O. I'm a barbarian, I guess.

(She checks her watch.)

Listen, I've gotta be someplace, so –

(**RAE** *rises.*)

RAE. Of course, I didn't mean to keep you.

(**RAE** *makes to go.*)

O. Was there something specific you wanted?

RAE. *(light)* Oh no. I just wanted to say hello.

O. Hello?

RAE. I just thought I'd swing by and see how everything
worked out for you.

(**O** *displays herself and her surroundings with a flourish.*)

O. Well? Not bad, eh?

RAE. Mm. Mm-hm.

O. It's not a mental hospital, is it? After all? It's not an
underpass. It's not a prison. It's not an unmarked
grave. It's just a nice apartment in a nice neighbor-
hood in the most beautiful borough of New York City.
Happy ending.

RAE. I don't know if "nice" is the *first* word I'd use, but –

O. *(cutting her off)* Yeah, okay.

RAE. But it's fine! I was going to say it's just fine.

O. I've gotta run. But thanks for swinging by.

    (on her way out)

    You can go out the way you came in.

    *(***O*** *exits. Lights shift.)*

Scene Eight

*(**REBECCA** in session, edgy, sitting as if she will, at the slightest provocation, spring up from her chair. **THE THERAPIST** across from her, poised and relaxed.)*

REBECCA. Okay.

(She swallows.)

It starts out with me on the 7. It's rush hour, it's crowded, I'm going home from work. The door at the far end of the car blows opens and some guy lurches in. I assume it's the accordion man coming to play his polka version of "Time in a Bottle" like he does every evening, but I look up and it's a Kontroller, a ticket checker like they have on the trains in Germany. The door bangs shut behind him, and he says, *"Papieren, bitte,"* and suddenly I realize that everyone on the car is German. We took a turn at Hunters Point and we're on the U-Bahn in West Berlin. As the Kontroller comes through the car towards me all the Germans produce their documents of purity and belonging, their passports and their pedigrees and the deeds to their ancestral homes or whatever, and he comes to me, and his eye is so blue it gives off a pale light, and his breath and his body smell like mint, and I put my hand into my pocket and there's this great raggedy hole where my wallet should be, and I realize that all my mongrel ID must have dropped out on the street somewhere back in Kreuzberg, or Chelsea. The eye of the German scans my face, and before I am able to explain what has happened he says, *"Aussteigen, bitte,"* and as the train slows into the station I get up without objection and move towards the door, and the German enfolds me in this...mist...of rebuke, and none of the other passengers can see me anymore.

(breath)

And then, when he leads me out onto the platform, and I can't pay the fine because my wallet is gone – I can't pay the fine because my wallet is gone! – he takes me to the place where Germans take Jews who don't follow the rules.

THE THERAPIST. Where do you think this dream comes from?

(beat)

REBECCA. That's it? "Where do you think this dream comes from"? That's what you've got for me?

THE THERAPIST. Well, what is it you want?

(REBECCA sighs.)

REBECCA. I want my hundred and twenty-five bucks back, please.

(Lights shift.)

Scene Nine

(Twilight. Moonrise. O and **REBECCA** *on the floor in a tangle of blankets, pillows, laundry. As they talk, as they kiss, O relieves* **REBECCA** *of her day-job outfit.)*

O. I fixed the ceiling today. While you were at work.

(They kiss.)

REBECCA. *You* fixed it? With what?

O. Packing tape.

*(***REBECCA** *moans – sexual, annoyed.)*

(responding to **REBECCA***'s moan)*

What? It worked. It's not dripping anymore.

(They kiss. They roll over, **REBECCA** *on top.)*

REBECCA. It's not dripping anymore because it's not raining anymore. I told you to call a roofer, a real roofing guy. The whole thing is going to –

(O and **REBECCA** *moan deeply, simultaneously.)*

…collapse…

O. No, it won't.

(They kiss. They roll over, O *on top.)*

It'll hold. It's a beautiful job. You should see what a beautiful job I did.

(O begins to fuck **REBECCA***, serious about it, attentive.* **REBECCA** *closes her eyes)*

REBECCA. Yes. Yes.

O. I'm amazing around the house.

REBECCA. You are. You're so handy.

(They kiss.)

O. Tell me about my skills.

REBECCA. Oh god, you're so skillful.

O. Yes. Tell me.

REBECCA. *(breathless)* The way you – the way you – plug up
   mouse holes –

O. Yes –

REBECCA. – and spackle cracks –

O. Yes –

REBECCA. – and ground outlets –

O. Yes –

REBECCA. It makes me want to –

O. Yes –

REBECCA. It makes me want to –

O. Yes –

REBECCA. Please – O – harder – please! Oh, yes!

> *(From somewhere deep inside the tangle of clothes and
> blankets, a cell phone rings.)*

> Oh, fuck!

> (**REBECCA** *twists away from* **O.***)*

O. What are you doing?!

> *(The cell phone chirps insistently as* **REBECCA** *tears
> through the jumble of clothes and blankets trying to find
> it.)*

> Leave it! Let it go!

REBECCA. One sec one sec don't hang up don't hang up –

> (**REBECCA** *finds the cell phone, beeps it on.)*

> *(into the phone)*

> Hello? Hi, Mom. Yeah.

> (**O** *collapses backwards onto the floor with a groan.*
> **REBECCA** *covers the mouthpiece.)*

> *(to* **O***) Shh!*

> *(breathless, into the phone)*

> Nothing. No, I wasn't. I wasn't running, I was…read-
> ing.

(O *crawls across the room to the dresser. She pulls open the bottom drawer and rummages through it noisily.*)

REBECCA. *(cont.) (into the phone)* Hang on a sec.

(covering the mouthpiece, a fierce whisper)

Could you be quiet, please?

(O *rolls her eyes.* REBECCA *turns her back to* O. O *retrieves what she's been looking for from the drawer: the Polaroid camera. She closes the drawer gently, crawls back to* REBECCA.)

(into the phone)

No, please don't tell her that, please. Because, I don't want to meet her son Alan. Because I just don't, I already told you, we had a discussion about this at –

(O *taps* REBECCA *on the shoulder.*)

Hang on a sec. Sorry.

(REBECCA *covers the mouthpiece, turns around.* O *takes a picture – flash!* REBECCA *winces.*)

O. "Rebecca Makes Nice to Mommy."

(REBECCA *glares at* O. O *presses her hand to her mouth to keep from giggling.*)

REBECCA. *(whisper) Stop. It.*

(back on the phone)

Hi. No, the doorbell just buzzed. Nobody. Why would I make that up? Somebody accidentally hit our buzzer.

(beat)

I said, somebody accidentally hit my buzzer. Mom, things are a little, why don't I call you tomorrow? Because I'm, why don't I just *call* you *tomorrow*? Yes I'll leave it on. Yes, I will. Yes I will. Okay. You, too. Bye.

(REBECCA *beeps off the phone, seriously unamused.* O *cracks up helplessly.*)

Why would you do that to me? You think that's funny?

O. Kind of, actually.

REBECCA. It's not funny. See how I'm not laughing?

O. I do see that, yes. But look at me: I'm laughing for the both of us.

REBECCA. Fuck you.

(REBECCA starts to gather up her clothes. She pulls her shirt back on, stands up, shimmies into her skirt. O chucks the camera aside, pursues her.)

O. *(still giggling)* Spookie, no, I'm sorry. I was just kidding, don't leave.

(O tries to drag REBECCA back down to the floor, REBECCA shakes her off.)

Come on, Spook, I apologize.

(throwing herself onto her stomach)

Look. Look. I'm on the floor. Look at me, I'm prostrate before you. Please let me finish what I started.

REBECCA. Sorry.

(REBECCA exits through the stage right door.)

O. *(calling after her)* Where are you going?

REBECCA. *(from off)* To call the roofer.

(beat)

O. Traitor.

(Lights shift.)

Scene Ten

(Queensbound 7 train, 10:35 p.m. Rush and clatter. The car is empty except for **REBECCA**, *who sits with her World War II research spread out across her lap, and* **THE LONELY NAZI**, *a young, piercingly attractive hipster guy — wire-rimmed glasses, black pea coat, black messenger bag, square-toed black patent leather shoes.)*

*(***THE LONELY NAZI*** stands above* **REBECCA**, *hanging onto a metal bar, peering down at her. They sway in tandem with the rocking of the train like undersea plants in the current. The train slows and comes to a halt — they lurch simultaneously. Sound of doors opening, the garbled PA announces, almost unintelligibly, that this is the last stop in Manhattan.)*

*(***REBECCA*** looks up,* **THE LONELY NAZI** *smiles down at her. She quickly looks back at her research material, shifts a few inches down the bench away from* **THE LONELY NAZI**.*)*

(Ding, ding. Sound of doors closing.)

(The train starts moving again. Again they sway in rhythm. **THE LONELY NAZI** *sits down beside* **REBECCA**.*)*

THE LONELY NAZI. *(just a ghost of a German accent)* I can't help noticing what it is that you are reading.

*(***REBECCA*** doesn't acknowledge this.)*

I also have an interest in this subject. As a coincidence.

*(***REBECCA*** doesn't look at him.)*

Are you maybe working on a project that concerns this subject?

*(***REBECCA*** blinks several times, then looks at him directly.)*

REBECCA. Yes. But I don't really feel like talking about it. Thanks.

THE LONELY NAZI. Áha.

(He folds his hands in his lap. They sway.)

I'm sorry to bother you again, but you might be strongly interested in the perspective I can offer you on these events.

REBECCA. *(not looking at him)* I don't think so.

*(**THE LONELY NAZI** gestures to a photograph in the book open in **REBECCA**'s lap.)*

THE LONELY NAZI. *(proudly)* Who is that, then?

*(**REBECCA** looks at the photograph, back at **THE LONELY NAZI**, astonished, deeply creeped.)*

REBECCA. What – ?

THE LONELY NAZI. That is, yes, me with my friends Dirk and Utz from the Einsatzgruppe. Three days from Leipzig, when that photo was taken.

REBECCA. *(flustered, vaguely trying to gather her stuff)* I'm sorry, I –

THE LONELY NAZI. Wait, please. Don't be upset.

REBECCA. I really think I'd – just – rather not.

THE LONELY NAZI. You're worried because I appear not to have aged since 1942.

*(**REBECCA** laughs, a little hysterically.)*

REBECCA. Uh, no, that wasn't really my first concern.

THE LONELY NAZI. You've never met an actual Nazi before.

REBECCA. *(playing along)* Well, that's true. So few of you around anymore.

THE LONELY NAZI. *(seriously)* Oh, no, not so. Not so at all. My workplace, for example. There are several of us in the office, including even my team leader, but we go, how does one say, *incognito*. It would be difficult, yes impossible to express the truth of our situation to co-workers. In this place, in this time period, people often react badly. As a result, we are very isolated.

(beat)

THE LONELY NAZI. *(cont.)* But you, I could tell, were different. I could tell you had a special interest.

REBECCA. It's not like a personal interest, it's a work assignment.

THE LONELY NAZI. And what is your work?

REBECCA. Children's books. Historical books. For schools.

THE LONELY NAZI. And you're teaching the children what about us? May I see?

(**THE LONELY NAZI** *reaches for* **REBECCA**'s *materials. She moves them away from him.*)

REBECCA. Uh, no, I don't think so.

THE LONELY NAZI. Please. I'm so interested. Read something to me. A small piece.

(**REBECCA** *considers him. He smiles dazzlingly.*)

REBECCA. About you?

THE LONELY NAZI. About anything.

(**REBECCA** *flips through her notebook dubiously, finds a passage.*)

REBECCA. *(reading)* "The Nazi soldiers were conditioned to believe Hitler's racist theories about Aryan superiority."

(**REBECCA** *looks at him.* **THE LONELY NAZI** *nods thoughtfully. She keeps going.*)

"The belief that Germans were the acme of human evolution allowed the Nazi soldiers to carry out atrocities against Jews, gypsies and other non-German racial and ethnic groups."

THE LONELY NAZI. *(searchingly)* This is, of course, true, but it doesn't capture the…feeling of it.

REBECCA. They're seventh graders reading this. I don't want to capture the "feeling" of atrocities.

THE LONELY NAZI. Oh, no, you mistake me. The feeling of the Nazi soldiers themselves. You want the students to understand both sides of the story.

REBECCA. Uh, I don't really think there are two sides.

THE LONELY NAZI. *(indignant)* But of course there are! Always, always there are, but especially in this case. Most especially here. In order for them to see what made the Bad Times occur, you must show them what it felt like to be in the Party.

REBECCA. I don't think that's really the point of the book, to teach kids how great it felt to be a Nazi.

THE LONELY NAZI. But you can't, you can't imagine it. So many fail to understand the way it gave us a reason, and brought us together as a people, as friends. And then, when it was over, we lost ourselves. We would see each other on the street, our eyes would connect, but we could not even speak each other's names out loud. "Forget everything," they said when they re-educated us. "That person who was you is not you anymore." It was as if we were all reborn as babies, but with a whole life of secrets trapped in each baby's heart.

(beat)

Do you see? Do you see why you must tell about us?

(The train begins to slow.)

REBECCA. *(alarmed)* I don't – . This isn't – . This is my stop.

THE LONELY NAZI. *(looking around)* Really?

REBECCA. *(gathering her belongings)* Yeah. Sorry.

(She gathers her belongings hastily.)

THE LONELY NAZI. I did not think this was your stop. I thought you debarked at the Woodside station.

REBECCA. *(low voice)* What?

THE LONELY NAZI. *(stiffly flirtatious)* Yes, I have noticed you. I have seen you on this train before.

(REBECCA gets up, looks around her in vain for other passengers.)

REBECCA. I gotta go.

(THE LONELY NAZI stands, pursues her.)

THE LONELY NAZI. May I walk you to your home?

REBECCA. No!

THE LONELY NAZI. I feel that we have much more to talk about.

REBECCA. Please, just leave me alone.

(Sound of doors opening, a garbled PA announcement. **REBECCA** *is out of there.)*

THE LONELY NAZI. *(calling after her)* I have no interest in hurting you! I only want you to understand everything there is to understand!

(Ding, ding. Lights shift.)

Scene Eleven

(Late night. The kitchenette, down right of the bedroom.
O *has held dinner for* **REBECCA**'s *return. Take-out*
containers all over the table. **O** *circles* **REBECCA** *once,*
considering her. She sits.)

O. *(shooting for cheerful)* It's so late. I was just a little worried about you.

REBECCA. *(distracted)* Yeah, the trains were, delayed.

O. Oh, yeah. They were?

REBECCA. Yeah. The 7 was.

O. What a pain.

REBECCA. Yeah, I waited forever.

(Pause. They chew.)

Wow, this is really good.

O. Yeah, it is, isn't it.

REBECCA. Is this from the Korean Mexican place?

O. No, this is from the Bengali Mexican place.

REBECCA. Oh, they're so great. I love them there.

O. I know. They're so nice.

REBECCA. Yeah.

O. They know my name.

REBECCA. Oh, really? They call you 'O' down there?

O. No, they call me 'Carlos.' I always give my secret code name when I'm ordering take-out.

REBECCA. That's so funny. 'Carlos.'

(A smiling, uncomfortable pause, with chewing. Finally)

O. Is something wrong?

REBECCA. *(heavy innocence)* No, why?

O. I don't know. You were late, and now you seem kind of – distracted.

REBECCA. Do I? I don't.

O. Yeah, you seem kind of – weird. Did something happen at work today?

REBECCA. *(immediately)* No.

O. Are you sure?

REBECCA. Yes, I'm sure nothing happened at work today.

O. Did your boss come down on you about your deadline or something?

REBECCA. No, I said, nothing happened at work today.

O. Did your mom call to bug you about Alan again?

REBECCA. *(snappish)* No, she didn't. I said nothing *happened.* I'm *fine.*

O. *(backing off)* Okay. Sorry.

(*beat*)

REBECCA. It was just a long day with the Nazis, that's all.

(**O** *softens.*)

O. I'm sorry. Poor Spook. I didn't mean to – interrogate you.

REBECCA. I know, I just – . I don't know how much more of this time period I can take. I think it's starting to mess with my mind.

O. Well, why wouldn't it.

REBECCA. Nobody really knows what happened then, you know? I mean everybody knows about it, but hardly anybody really *knows* about it, like deeply, and these kids, when they get done with my book, they're not really going to know a thing about it, either. They want me to put word scrambles in the Auschwitz Unit.

O. You're kidding.

REBECCA. *(rising agitation)* I can't go too far or I'll freak them out. I can't be too tame or I won't cover the state-mandated curriculum. The result is a piece of total bullshit.

O. *(nicely)* No, Spookie, I'm sure –

REBECCA. *(overlapping)* No, it is, it's a total disgrace what I'm doing. You were right. There's not one authentic thing in it. I'm producing a giant bundle of lies. And then this guy, this guy on the 7 train –

O. *(too quick)* What guy? What happened?

(REBECCA peers at O.)

REBECCA. Nothing. It's nothing.

O. What's nothing? What happened? Are you okay?

REBECCA. Of course I am. There was just, this guy started asking me questions –

O. About what?

REBECCA. You know, it was really no big deal.

O. Was he like, macking on you?

REBECCA. *(precise)* No, O. He was not "macking" on me.

O. Are you sure?

REBECCA. *(now sarcastic)* Yes, I'm sure he wasn't "macking" on me.

O. Well, did you have like a conversation with him?

REBECCA. It doesn't even matter.

O. What did you talk about?

REBECCA. O…

O. No, cause I'm just curious what you talked about with this cute guy on the 7.

REBECCA. Did I say he was cute?

O. Well wasn't he?

(Beat. REBECCA shakes her head.)

REBECCA. You are completely, totally nuts. Nothing happened, it was just supposed to be a funny story. I'm sorry I brought it up.

(REBECCA goes pointedly back to eating. O crosses to the counter, gets the Polaroid camera, returns to her seat. She aims the camera at REBECCA across the table.)

You know, this joke is really starting to get on my nerves.

O. *(quiet)* This? Is not a joke. This is documentation.

(REBECCA stares levelly into the camera's eye. O takes a picture of her – flash! – lowers the camera.)

"Rebecca Tells Me a Funny Story."

(Lights shift.)

Scene Twelve

(**REBECCA** *in writing light.*)

REBECCA. *(evenly)* Recognizing True and False Statements. Based on what you have read so far, circle the statements in the following list that are *not* true. One. Germany during the Third Reich was a totalitarian state. Two. Adolf Hitler was well known for his charismatic public speaking style. Three. The Nuremberg Laws were a series of statutes designed to protect Jews from discrimination. Four. Jews in the Lódz and Warsaw ghettoes were housed in comfortable, four-star accommodations prior to their deportation to the East. Five. Many Jews failed to leave Germany until it was too late because they believed their German friends would protect them from persecution. Six. Once the killings began, many Jews collaborated with Nazi officials in the hopes of increasing their own chance of survival.

Scene Thirteen

(O on the floor by the bed, next to a heap of wood scraps, swatches and paint chips, slipping photographs into a photo album. RAE sits thoughtfully on the bed behind her.)

RAE. I lived in an apartment once.

(O jumps, startled.)

O. God, you scared me. What are you doing here?

RAE. I was just saying that I lived in apartment, too, once, after Bryn Mawr, before Daddy.

O. I didn't know there *was* an after Bryn Mawr, before Daddy.

RAE. There was. A short interval.

O. I thought you met Daddy at your sophomore year mixer.

RAE. I did.

O. And you were married the June after you graduated.

RAE. Yes, we were.

O. So a very short interval.

RAE. A short, bright interval.

(RAE slips off her pumps and stretches out comfortably on the bed, Grace-Kelly-in-Rear-Window-style.)

It was with another girl, Mary Ellen I-forget-her-last-name, in an apartment in Washington, D.C. Her father kept the place for business trips, and Mary Ellen had a determination to work at the Library of Congress, and she was looking for someone to share the place with, and I remember we were out on the green in front of our dormitory on the first truly springish day that last April, and she was mentioning this to a group of us, about the apartment, and before I had any notion that I was going to do it I had volunteered to join her. I heard myself say, "I've always wanted to work in government," which was ridiculous, I might as well have said, "I've always wanted to sprout feathers and fly like

a pigeon," for all that was true. And then the chorus
of the other girls: "But what about Harold? What
about the wedding?" Half of them had already had
their bridesmaid's gowns fitted. And like a woman pos-
sessed I heard myself say, "I believe things are ending
with Harold. It's been ending between us for some
time now," and there were shouts and cries and such
a ruckus, but suddenly it was all arranged, and when
Daddy came to pick me up for Saturday I told him it
was over.

O. I never heard this. I never heard anything about this.

RAE. Well, it wasn't a story Daddy liked me to tell, after he
came to D.C. and all but kidnapped me back to him in
time for the wedding. He felt it made us look...unreli-
able.

O. Well, it basically does.

RAE. Do you know that every room in that place Mary
Ellen had painted a different shade of yellow? An
ochre-yellow hallway and a canary-yellow living room
and a lemon-yellow kitchenette. The bathroom was
an appropriate mustard color. My room was saffron,
Oriental, in a way – Turkish. And when the sun would
stream in through those long tall windows the whole
place went up like stained glass, everything glowed. It
was like living inside a daffodil.

(O *looks into the middle distance, seeing it.*)

O. That must have been nice.

(RAE *leans over* O*'s shoulder to look at the photograph
still in* O*'s hand.*)

RAE. Is that your, friend?

(O *snaps back to the present.*)

O. (*preparing to scold*) She's not my –

RAE. (*cutting her off*) Yes, yes, spare me the vocabulary lesson.
What's she *doing* there?

O. Changing a lightbulb, I think.

(O *and* RAE *peer at the photograph.*)

RAE. She looks lovely. She looks responsible.

O. She is.

RAE. She's not much like your first one, is she?

O. I don't want to talk about that.

RAE. What a horror show that was.

O. I said I don't want to discuss it.

RAE. I'm just saying you're moving up in the world! It's a compliment. She's beautiful.

O. Look, this is my house. If you're not going to follow my rules, I'm going to have to throw you out.

RAE. You don't have to be melodramatic about it. I can't stay anyway, I was just passing through.

(RAE *makes to go.*)

But you're about to make a big mistake with that slate grey, you don't have the light for it in here, it'll be like living in a cave. Something brighter—ecru? Even true white.

(RAE *vanishes.*)

O. – Really?

(O *looks around for* RAE. *Lights shift.*)

Scene Fourteen

(Midnight. Deserted city darkness. Sliver-moon small and high in the sky, patchy clouds. Ghost skyline – no hard edges.)

(The bedroom, as dark as it ever gets. Zero visual, the sounds of sex.)

REBECCA. *(unseen, from out of the darkness)* Oh God, *no.* I mean, yes.

O. *(unseen, from out of the darkness)* No?

REBECCA. Yes. Oh. Oh!

O. No?

REBECCA. *Yes.*

*(In the dark, **REBECCA** makes contact with a foreign object.)*

(suddenly) Ow! What's –

O. *(hopeful)* Yes? Can I –

REBECCA. What – what –

O. Do you –

REBECCA. Wait –

O. Please?

REBECCA. I don't know, I'm not –

O. Please.

(pause)

REBECCA. *(bravely)* Okay. Yes. Okay.

O. Just *say*, if it –

REBECCA. I know.

O. Just *say.*

REBECCA. Okay.

(There's a pause. Weird shuffling-around noises, klutzy getting-things-set-up noises, standing-on-the-bed noises.)

(suddenly) Ow –

O. Oh, sorry, was that your –

REBECCA. No, no, it's okay.

O. I'm so sorry, I didn't mean to –

REBECCA. It's fine, it's okay.

(*silence – readymaking*)

O. Okay?

REBECCA. Yes.

O. Now?

REBECCA. (*breathy, anticipatory*) Yes.

(O *photographs* REBECCA *– flash! In the darkness that follows,* REBECCA *sits bolt upright.*)

REBECCA. What the *fuck*?

O. I thought you said –

REBECCA. You brought that fucking thing into *bed* with us?

O. I thought you – I'm sorry, I thought –

(REBECCA *flips on the bedside light, sits huddled on the far side of the bed from* O, *holding the covers to her chest.*)

REBECCA. I didn't think you were gonna do *that*, I thought –

O. What did you *think* I was gonna –

REBECCA. I just –

O. What did you – you thought –

REBECCA. (*ashamed*) I don't know, I thought it was –

(*A look crosses* O*'s face.*)

O. What, you thought –

REBECCA. No!

O. Without even – Jesus, who do you think I *am*?

REBECCA. I think you're the kind of person who takes naked pictures of people without asking their permission!

O. I *did* ask your permission.

REBECCA. I didn't know you were asking permission for *that*.

O. No, you thought I was asking if I could –

REBECCA. (*cutting her off, insistent*) I don't *know* what I thought you were asking me for.

*(Pause. **REBECCA** turns away from **O**, discreetly pulls on a robe.)*

O. *(quiet)* Why don't you just admit what you like?

REBECCA. *(miserable)* I can't.

O. I'd do it. If you would just ask me for it I'd do it.

REBECCA. *("trust me")* No, you wouldn't.

O. Yes, I would. I want to.

REBECCA. Forget it.

*(**REBECCA** gets up.)*

O. *(pleading)* I want to be what you want me to be. I *love* you.

*(**REBECCA** gives **O** a look.)*

(taken aback) I do.

*(**REBECCA** crosses stage left, heading for the bathroom.)*

You're always on your way out.

REBECCA. I'm just going to brush my teeth.

*(**REBECCA** exits. A beat.)*

O. *(half to herself)* Why don't you just leave me now, before it gets ugly.

*(**REBECCA** reenters with two toothbrushes prepped with paste.)*

REBECCA. I'm not going to leave you.

O. *(simply)* I know you are.

*(**REBECCA** sighs, hands **O** one of the toothbrushes.)*

REBECCA. Honey, brush.

*(**REBECCA** sits down next to **O** on the edge of the bed. For a beat they brush their teeth together in silence. Slowly, **REBECCA** leans her head onto **O**'s shoulder. They brush for a beat in this position.)*

(through her toothbrush)

I love you, too.

(Lights shift.)

Scene Fifteen

(**REBECCA** *in writing light.*)

REBECCA. *(evenly)* Understanding Reasons. In-class project. Fold a piece of looseleaf paper in half lengthwise, forming two columns. In Column One, print the following sentence fragments taken from the previous chapter, skipping a line between each one:

Historically, totalitarian states arise out of pluralistic democracies because

Hitler's public displays of brutality were attractive to many ordinary Germans because

By 1941, fully eighty-five percent of German citizens were members of the Nazi Party because

(beat)

Next, obtain a hall pass from your social studies teacher. Find a quiet place where you can be alone, perhaps a supply closet or faculty restroom. Sit down on the floor of your quiet place and lean your head back against the cinderblock wall. Stare at the blank lines of Column Two until the time left on your hall pass runs out.

(A subway train approaches, grows louder. Lights shift.)

Scene Sixteen

(The subway noise reaches a pitch and holds.)

(10:40 p.m. **REBECCA** *on the 7 train home, reading "Martha Stewart Living." The train slows, stops.* **REBECCA** *lurches. Sound of doors opening.)*

*(***THE EAGER NAZI** *bounds onto the car. He is J. Crewsporty: logoless baseball cap, V-neck shirt with stripes down each sleeve, aerodynamic running shoes, duffelstyle gym bag. Garbled PA announcement:* Last stop in Manhattan, next stop Vernon-Jackson Road in Queens.*)*

(Ding, ding. Sound of doors closing. **REBECCA** *and* **THE EAGER NAZI** *sway with the motion of the moving train.)*

*(***THE EAGER NAZI** *crosses to* **REBECCA** *and peers aggressively into her face.)*

THE EAGER NAZI. Excuse me!

*(***REBECCA** *hesitates a beat.)*

REBECCA. Yes?

THE EAGER NAZI. *(square grin; strong German accent)* Hello! Tell me please, does this train go to the Shea Stadium, home of the New York Mets of the National Baseball League?

*(***REBECCA** *perceives his accent, debates with herself a beat.)*

REBECCA. Yes.

(She returns to her magazine.)

THE EAGER NAZI. Thank you very much wait a moment please, when will I know that we have arrived in the station for the Shea Stadium?

REBECCA. It'll say "Shea Stadium" on it. Or actually it'll say "Citi Field," it's not called Shea Stadium anymore.

(She returns to her magazine again.)

THE EAGER NAZI. Ah, interesting. Thank you very much!

(He sits down beside her. Beat. They sway.)

You are also traveling to the Shea Stadium?

(REBECCA *doesn't hear him, because she doesn't or because she doesn't care to.* **THE EAGER NAZI** *leans towards her.)*

(louder) You also travel to the Shea Stadium?!

(REBECCA *sighs, looks up.)*

REBECCA. No.

THE EAGER NAZI. But you are a supporter of the New York Mets?

REBECCA. No.

THE EAGER NAZI. *(confused, pointing to her scarf and a stripe on her bag)* But you are wearing I see both orange and blue.

(REBECCA *is nonplussed by this.)*

REBECCA. I don't really have an opinion about the Mets one way or the other.

THE EAGER NAZI. *(wounded)* But you must make a choice: New York Yankees or New York Mets. You are a New Yorker, yes? All those who live in New York must make a choice. Then you show devotion to your chosen organization by displaying the colors on hats or shirts or perhaps pants.

(He gestures, an explanation.)

Orange, and blue. I am going now to the Shea Stadium to buy some items to display my devotion to the New York Mets, because I have chosen to support the Mets and not the Yankees.

REBECCA. Um, are you a tourist?

THE EAGER NAZI. *(defensive)* No, I am a New Yorker!

REBECCA. Well, you know, it's kind of late at night. I don't think they're gonna be open right now. Plus it's winter. Baseball season doesn't start until spring.

THE EAGER NAZI. *(deflated)* Ah.

(reinvigorated, indignant)

But I see everywhere people walking with displays of devotion to Mets and Yankees.

REBECCA. Well that's because you can get that stuff anywhere. You can get it in any little sidewalk shop in Manhattan. You didn't have to come all the way out here on the 7.

(**THE EAGER NAZI** *smiles heartily, like he's received his cue.*)

THE EAGER NAZI. Ah, but I am not sorry I have come here on the 7, because if I do not come here on the 7 I will not meet you.

(**REBECCA** *blushes in spite of herself and smiles briefly, with only the edges of her lips.*)

REBECCA. *(dumbly)* Oh. Well. Thank you.

(**THE EAGER NAZI** *shifts towards* **REBECCA** *on the bench.*)

THE EAGER NAZI. *(confidentially)* You have put me this question over whether I am a New Yorker or not. I must explain that I work very hard to be blended with the natural New Yorkers, but I am yes from Germany originally.

REBECCA. *(polite)* Really.

THE EAGER NAZI. I am from Bautzen, home of the world-famous Bautzen Mustard. We are a very small town but we make the very big mustard.

REBECCA. Huh. But you live in New York now?

THE EAGER NAZI. I have for many years lived in New York. I study now to be a tour guide on the New York tourist bus. I like to work outdoors, where I can feel the wind blowing me.

(**REBECCA** *smiles.*)

REBECCA. That sounds nice.

THE EAGER NAZI. Do you like also to work outdoors?

REBECCA. Um, yeah, I guess. I mean, I'm in publishing, so I don't really get the chance to –

THE EAGER NAZI. *(interrupting, irrepressible)* In my youth group they instructed us the value of sport and fresh air and comradeship. In the forest together we climbed on rocks and slept in dirt, and we understood what does it mean to be strong and to belong to a group. Today we no longer sleep in dirt. Today we go to the Shea or the Yankee Stadium or we go perhaps to the bar and we watch other men make sport. But it is not enough for the heroes only to be strong: Alexander Rodriguez and Derek Jeter.

(He pronounces it "yeeter.")

The group becomes strong only when every boy in it is strong. That was the belief of our youth group.

*(**REBECCA** blinks at him.)*

REBECCA. What youth group is this?

THE EAGER NAZI. *Ha Jot.* Maybe you have heard of it.

*(A moment in which **REBECCA** processes her reaction to this: fear, embarrassment, excitement.)*

REBECCA. *Hitlerjugend.* I've heard of it, yeah.

THE EAGER NAZI. This was before I came to New York.

REBECCA. *(baleful)* It would have to be.

THE EAGER NAZI. We made sporting events, and camping excursions, and bonfires –

REBECCA. *(echo)* Bonfires…

THE EAGER NAZI. *(wistful)* We made sometimes bonfires *at* sporting events…

*(**REBECCA** puts her copy of "Martha Stewart Living" down on the bench beside her, pivots to face **THE EAGER NAZI**.)*

REBECCA. Can I ask you a question?

THE EAGER NAZI. Of course.

REBECCA. You were a youth in the Hitler Youth, the Hitler Youth was disbanded, what, I don't have the exact date, sometime in –

THE EAGER NAZI. *(vehemently)* May 8, 1945.

(beat)

REBECCA. Right. Which makes you...

THE EAGER NAZI. *(in his tourist bus voice)* The moment was coming and we knew it was coming although we hoped it would not come, but we did not fear it, and when it came we remained strong. The clock ran down to zero and they ended us, but we were not afraid.

*(leaning in to **REBECCA**)*

I smell that you are afraid, all the time.

REBECCA. Me? No. Of what?

(He sniffs her aggressively – she shrinks back.)

THE EAGER NAZI. But I smell also courage. When it is time it will become, yes, so *easy.*

(looking her dead in the eye)

When time runs out every decision is justified.

(Garbled PA announcement: Next stop, Vernon-Jackson Road. *The train begins to slow into the station.)*

I think I will go rather back to Manhattan, to look for displays in the sidewalk shops you explained me.

(He indicates her copy of "Martha Stewart Living.")

Excuse me, is it finished?

REBECCA. Huh? Sure, go ahead.

THE EAGER NAZI. Thank you, I am interested.

*(**THE EAGER NAZI** picks up the magazine, crosses to the subway door. He opens the magazine, peers into it, gasps in delight.)*

*(Sound of train grinding to a halt. **REBECCA** and **THE EAGER NAZI** lurch. **THE EAGER NAZI** holds the magazine open for her to see.)*

THE EAGER NAZI. *(cont.)* *(thrilled)* Pillows – made from *hand-kerchiefs!*

(Sound of doors opening. **THE EAGER NAZI** *leaps from the car. Ding, ding. Lights shift. The sound of the subway train recedes.)*

Scene Seventeen

(Silence. **REBECCA** *in session, holding her briefcase against her chest like a shield. She sits completely still, waiting.* **THE THERAPIST** *watches her calmly.)*

*(***REBECCA** *opens her mouth, lets it hang open, closes it.)*

*(***THE THERAPIST** *cocks her head curiously.* **REBECCA** *leans forward slightly in her chair, holds a second, re-reclines.* **THE THERAPIST** *raises her eyebrows slightly.)*

THE THERAPIST. Anytime you're ready.

REBECCA. Okay.

(beat)

So what do you say to people who start…

(healthy pause)

THE THERAPIST. Start what?

REBECCA. *(quiet)* Right. If I tell you, you'll think I'm crazy.

THE THERAPIST. No…

REBECCA. Yes, you will, because it's fucking *insane* what's been going on in my head. It's fucking *lunacy*, and if I tell you you're going to commit me –

THE THERAPIST. No, I won't…

REBECCA. *(continuous)* – and strap me down to some plastic cot and put a rubber bit in my mouth and sizzle me with a thousand volts like you did to Sylvia Plath, and –

THE THERAPIST. *(overlapping)* Like *I* did to Sylvia Plath?

REBECCA. – I'll never be the same person again and I'll eventually give in to despair and kill myself by putting my head in the oven and who wants *that*? Who *wants* that?

THE THERAPIST. I certainly don't.

REBECCA. Thank you. All right. I'm not going to tell you.

(beat)

THE THERAPIST. You know, I'm an M.S.W. I'm not licensed to give anybody electroshock therapy. There is absolutely no risk to you of me giving you electroshock therapy, no matter what you say to me.

(beat)

Does that make you feel safer?

REBECCA. *(disconsolate)* Hardly.

*(**REBECCA** puts her head down on her briefcase.)*

I'm sure they're symbolic of something. I mean, what isn't symbolic of something else? But on the other hand, they're so *real.* They're so, incredibly, real.

THE THERAPIST. What are?

REBECCA. The last one was so physically perfect, every single detail, right down to the downy hair on his cheek, his breath, his slightly sour coffee breath, the ridges on his front teeth…They're real. I can't explain it, but they're real.

THE THERAPIST. *(gently)* Who are "they"?

REBECCA. The Nazis.

THE THERAPIST. Nazis?

REBECCA. Actual, bona fide, World War II Nazis. Among us, apparently. On the 7 train. Weekdays, after 10 p.m.

THE THERAPIST. *(respectfully)* Wow.

REBECCA. I *know,* I thought they had all gone to, you know, Argentina or wherever, but apparently lots of them live in the outer boroughs, they appear to have infiltrated the oh my god, when I hear myself saying these things I don't even recognize my own voice.

THE THERAPIST. How does that make you feel?

REBECCA. *(with sudden vehemence)* Well it's O's *fault.*

THE THERAPIST. What does O have to do with you not recognizing your own voice?

REBECCA. *(overlapping)* No, it is, it's her, it's her apartment, know it. I never should have moved in with her. The place has spores drifting through it, and asbestos, some kind of gas, radon seeping out of the baseboards or something. I get headaches there. I don't trust myself there.

THE THERAPIST. Rebecca. Can we back up a minute, to the Nazis? You say you're being visited on the train by Nazis?

REBECCA. You know, you don't seem to appreciate what she's doing to me. I'm worse every time I come in here, but I don't see you picking up on that. I'm sorry to be so frank about it, but since we're on the subject it *is* actually starting to worry me that you don't notice these things. I mean, you are supposed to be a *therapist*, no offense.

THE THERAPIST. So you want to talk about the things I notice about you?

REBECCA. No, *listen*, God, nobody's listening to me. She turns all my loyalties upside down. I don't even know if I believe that I've done half the things I remember doing with her, because how could I have? The other night, with the –

(She flirts with the memory, dismisses it.)

– whatever, impossible. How could that have been me? Then again, how can there be Nazis on the 7? Things happen.

THE THERAPIST. I'd like to get back to those Nazis –

REBECCA. No, excuse me, this is *my* session and I want to talk about O.

(beat)

THE THERAPIST. We can talk about anything –

REBECCA. *(interrupting, nasty)* I know, we can talk about anything I want to talk about. Isn't this just the most perfect relationship. Don't I just have the world on a string in this room.

(THE THERAPIST breathes.)

૪૩ . Is there something you want to say to me
          ot saying?

(A blows out a hefty, put-upon sigh.)

ECCA. Actually, yes. Actually, now that you mention it,
   there's something very serious I've been wanting to say.

THE THERAPIST. All right.

REBECCA. I didn't want to shock you, or hurt your feelings,
   or make things awkward between us. That's why I held
   back. Until now.

THE THERAPIST. I'm listening.

REBECCA. I have to leave you.

THE THERAPIST. You mean terminate?

REBECCA. That's right, I have to terminate you.

THE THERAPIST. Okay. I have some thoughts about that, if
   you'll give me a second –

REBECCA. *(overlapping, wincingly apologetic)* Actually, wow, I
   really don't think talking it through is the right thing
   for me at this point. I actually feel really comfortable
   with my decision. In fact, I feel so comfortable with it
   that I think I'm going to forfeit the remainder of my
   session today.

THE THERAPIST. I don't know how I feel about that,
   actually –

REBECCA. Well I'm really comfortable with that decision,
   too, actually, so I think I'm just going to follow through
   on it and, you know, get the hell out of here.

   *(**REBECCA** gets up.)*

THE THERAPIST. I really think it would be better if we talked
   about this –

REBECCA. *(overlapping)* I don't think so, but thanks a lot,
   though, really. You've been a big help. An incredible
   help. I swear.

   *(**REBECCA** ducks out. **THE THERAPIST** gets up from her
   chair.)*

THE THERAPIST. Rebecca –

   (Lights shift.)

Scene Eighteen

(The bedroom, dishwater-gray early morning light. **REBECCA** *and* O *offstage in the bathroom.)*

REBECCA. *(off)* I never said you could come.

O. *(off)* You said next time.

> *(***REBECCA** *enters, tense, pursued by* O, *in A-shirt and boxers.* **REBECCA** *circulates, readying herself for work between spasms of argument.)*

REBECCA. I said maybe.

O. You said "next time," I remember distinctly, you –

> *(From the pocket of her coat hanging by the door,* **REBECCA***'s cell phone begins to ring.* O *and* **REBECCA** *halt, look at the ringing coat. The phone rings once, twice.)*

Phone.

REBECCA. It's 7:30 in the morning. I'm not answering the phone at 7:30 in the morning.

O. Maybe it's urgent.

REBECCA. *(grimly)* It's not urgent.

> *(After two more rings, the phone shuts up. A beat, then* O *picks up exactly where she left off.)*

O. I remember distinctly that you –

REBECCA. *(overlapping)* You remember what you *wish* I had said, and I wish you would stop trying to pin this on me when you're just pissed because –

O. You won't let me into your *life*?

REBECCA. *(desperately)* What do you want from me?

O. I want you to invite me to lunch!

REBECCA. *(quiet)* I can't.

O. *(exploding)* Why? What is so *wrong* with me?

REBECCA. Please don't yell.

O. (O *takes it down a notch*) You think I'm gonna chew with my mouth open or something? I know you may find this hard to believe but I've eaten at restaurants with tablecloths before. I even know which fucking fork to use first.

REBECCA. That has nothing to do with it and you know it.

O. Then what *is* it?

(*In the coat by the door,* REBECCA*'s cell phone rings again.*)

Maybe she wants to change where you're meeting.

REBECCA. She can leave a message.

O. If you're not gonna answer it why don't you just turn it off?

REBECCA. I promised her I wouldn't.

O. But –

REBECCA. Just *ignore* it? Please?

(*The phone stops ringing.* REBECCA *returns to getting ready.*)

O. What if I just showed up?

REBECCA. You wouldn't do that.

O. I don't think I'm booked today.

(*She consults the datebook in her mind.*)

Yeah, no, I'm free for lunch, I'll swing by. El Azteco on 53rd?

REBECCA. Please don't do this to me.

O. Swing by and say hi to you and Lily.

REBECCA. Please *please* don't.

O. So now you're *begging* me not to come meet your mother.

REBECCA. Please, just, not right now.

O. When?

REBECCA. Later.

O. (*suddenly wild, louder and louder*) Never never *never!*

REBECCA. Please don't yell!

(**O** *paces.*)

(*coaxing, soothing*) Come on, you don't seriously want to come to El Azteco, do you? And like, sit there in your, in your –

(*She gestures at O's body.* **O** *looks down at her anti-outfit.*)

O. *What?*

REBECCA. *I* don't know, *you* know! Next to my mother? Eating guacamole? From the little stone bowl with feet?

O. Yes.

REBECCA. You think that could actually happen in real life?

O. Yes!

(**REBECCA** *turns away.*)

REBECCA. You don't know her. You don't know what she's like.

O. No, and whose fault is that?

(**REBECCA** *shrugs this off.*)

REBECCA. You don't get it.

O. Oh I get it, believe me, of all people I get it. It's hard. But you still owe it to her to tell her the truth.

REBECCA. And what is the truth?

O. Don't you know anymore?

REBECCA. You know, I love this thing where you get to set the moral standard for my life. Because you're clearly such a paragon of virtue.

O. I've never once lied about who I am.

REBECCA. No, and that's worked out great for you, hasn't it?

O. *(startled)* – What?

REBECCA. It must be nice to live in such a simple world. Your mother doesn't approve of your lifestyle choice? Well fuck *her*, she's the *oppressor*, who gives a *fuck* what she thinks. You obviously never gave a shit about how she feels. You broke her heart and you cut her off and you have no remorse about it and you call it "pride."

O. *(stunned)* Is *that* what you think the story is.

REBECCA. I *love* her. I have a *responsibility* to her. Sometimes you have to protect the people you love from the truth.

O. Although I guess *this* is not one of those times.

(In the coat pocket, REBECCA's cell phone rings.)

Mother*fuck*, I can't stand it anymore.

(O heads for the coat.)

REBECCA. Leave it.

O. I'm shutting it off.

REBECCA. No *leave* it! Let it go!

O. I'm gonna throw the fucking thing out!

REBECCA. Don't touch it! Don't touch it, O!

(O wrests the ringing cell phone free from the coat pocket. REBECCA dives for it, they fight for control of the phone – intense, physical. O holds it up out of REBECCA's reach, then hurls it, hard, into the garbage can. It lands with a thunk, stops ringing.)

(REBECCA crosses to the garbage can, picks up the phone gingerly. Opens it, holds it up to her ear.)

REBECCA. You're an animal.

O. I'm sorry –

REBECCA. It's dead. You killed it.

O. I'm sorry. That sucked. Spookie, that sucked.

(O moves towards REBECCA but she edges away, drops the phone back into the garbage can, gathers her coat and briefcase, shaky.)

Don't go. I'm sorry!

REBECCA. *(abstract)* I gotta go.

(REBECCA moves to the door.)

O. Don't walk away in the middle of this.

REBECCA. I gotta go.

(Lights shift.)

Scene Nineteen

REBECCA. *(even, pulsing with restraint)* Role Playing. Imagine a world not unlike your own.

Imagine that you are a seventh grader. You are well dressed and well rounded. No reasonable request you have ever made has been denied. You have never gone hungry a day in your life.

Now picture the downstairs of your suburban home. Imagine your mother in the kitchen making supper. Imagine your father on the couch watching the Accu-Weather forecast.

Imagine yourself, cross-legged beside him on the carpet, doing your homework. Doing this exercise.

Suddenly, a pair of heavily armed storm troopers bursts in from the patio, exploding through the sliding doors in a shower of glass. They have seen something ugly buried deep in your family, something hidden beneath the skin of your own pink, budding body. They are here to purge the world of what you represent.

They raise their weapons. Your father throws his arms over his head in a gesture of cowardice you never would have believed he was capable of. From the kitchen you hear your mother scream like a child.

The storm trooper with the bigger submachine gun approaches you, his boots sinking deep into the rug with each step. He comes closer to you and you feel your breath go quiet. His hatred of you fills the air like a fume.

You look up at him, into his eyes, and his vision sinks back into the vanishing point. That collapse into nothing at the center of his pupils exerts this strong gravitational pull, it makes you look and then it holds you there: the coldest, most exciting zero in the world.

In 500 words or less, about two double-spaced pages, describe the moment in which you feel yourself dissolve into his will. Destroy your response before your teacher, or anyone else, can see it.

(Lights shift.)

Scene Twenty

*(Queensbound 7 train, 10:45 p.m. **REBECCA**, coat and hat and scarf, sobbing to herself. She hunches over her briefcase, which is clutched in her lap.)*

*(At the other end of the bench is **THE TENDER NAZI**, dressed for benevolent weather. He is slender and boyish with a loose-fitting T-shirt, frayed jeans and Tevas, a jade amulet on a cord around his neck.)*

*(The train is in motion – the roar of the tunnel all around them. **REBECCA** and **THE TENDER NAZI** sway to the rhythm.)*

*(**THE TENDER NAZI** watches **REBECCA** sob for a moment, then moves closer to her. The most delicate German accent tints his English – a gel on a light.)*

THE TENDER NAZI. What's wrong?

*(**REBECCA** looks at him, knows immediately what his deal is.)*

REBECCA. I'm sobbing.

*(**REBECCA** snorts a messy snort, wipes her dripping face with the back of her hand. From the pocket of his jeans, **THE TENDER NAZI** produces a mini-pack of tissues. He extends them towards her.)*

THE TENDER NAZI. Would you like a Puffs Plus with aloe vera lotion?

REBECCA. Thank you.

*(She takes the whole pack, pulls all of the tissues out of the plastic wrapper and mops at her face with the wad of them. When she's done she looks around for a place to toss them, opens her briefcase and drops them inside. She snaps the briefcase shut, hunches back over. **THE TENDER NAZI** looks at her with raw concern.)*

THE TENDER NAZI. Why are you sobbing?

REBECCA. I am sobbing because. I am sobbing because at least six million people died in the Holocaust, and I wasn't there to save any of them. Their suffering is complete. It began, it ended, and thirty-five years later I arrived on the scene, helpless to prevent a single one of their deaths.

THE TENDER NAZI. *(serious)* Yes. That is a tragedy.

REBECCA. No, you can't say what it is. You can *say* "tragedy" or "horror" or "obscenity" about it, but using a word to describe this thing is like throwing a penny into a black hole. The event engulfs the word. There are no words.

THE TENDER NAZI. So you're sobbing because there are no words?

REBECCA. No. That's not why I'm sobbing.

(pause)

What happens to people when they study the Holocaust is that they go numb in the face of the figures, because how many is six million anyway? How many packed Shea Stadiums is that? How many Saint Patrick's Day Parades? I mean, New York is a city of twelve point five million people but you don't get a *sense* of those twelve point five million, there's no place in New York that could accommodate all twelve point five million New Yorkers at once. Really, it's a miracle the public transit system even works. When you think of the daily passenger volume it's staggering. The point is, you *live* New York one – freak at a time. So the old guy who elbows in front of you at the check-out and the bike messenger who does his war whoop in your ear and the crazy lady trying to sell you her hat on the subway platform – that's how you figure out what twelve point five million means. It's the same for the six million. People go, "Six million, six million, wow, that sucks." They can't get their mind around it. Then you read the story of the nine-year-old whose mother puts her on the Kindertransport train with a pretzel and a doll and a chalk mark on her coat and you just – cry.

(pause)

REBECCA. *(cont.)* I should have put more of those moments in the book. Maybe that's what they wanted. I tried, I just – I fucked up.

THE TENDER NAZI. You are writing a book about this?

REBECCA. I was. Until four thirty this afternoon.

(She begins to sob again.)

I'm sorry.

THE TENDER NAZI. Please, go ahead. Although my Puffs Plus with aloe vera lotion are gone.

REBECCA. Do you know what they re-assigned me to? Betsy fucking Ross: "She Sewed a Nation's Hopes." They were really nice about it, actually. They didn't fire me. They did make me give up my research, though. Four months of my work passed on to Artis Blythe, that smug Yalie bitch. So she can "pick up where I left off." The moment when they took my folders away was...

(She is overwhelmed; gathers herself.)

I mean, that's probably an indication that you've gotten too emotionally involved with your subject matter, if giving up your research materials feels like having your arm chopped off.

THE TENDER NAZI. *(sympathetic)* That is a very violent image.

(REBECCA looks at THE TENDER NAZI as if aware of his presence for the first time. She feels a rush of affection for him.)

REBECCA. You're being so nice to me. You don't have to be this nice.

THE TENDER NAZI. I feel bad.

REBECCA. What do you feel bad about?

THE TENDER NAZI. I feel bad about the things I did during the war.

(REBECCA sighs.)

REBECCA. You know, I've had a really hard day. If you think you're going to confess your sins to me and I'm going to *absolve* you or something –

THE TENDER NAZI. *(cutting her off)* I know you won't absolve me. No one can absolve me.

REBECCA. That's right. I don't know what you did, but that's right.

THE TENDER NAZI. You say it is hard to have been born too late to save people. Imagine how hard it is to have memories of killing them.

REBECCA. But see, you're dodging responsibility.

THE TENDER NAZI. I am not trying to dodge responsibility!

REBECCA. Even in the grammar of your sentence you're doing it. "Having memories of killing" is cleaner than actually killing.

THE TENDER NAZI. I have memories of killing because I killed.

REBECCA. Whatever.

THE TENDER NAZI. *(sorrowful)* People make terrible mistakes.

REBECCA. *(spitting out each word)* No, don't tell me it was a "mistake." An entire nation working together on a mass extermination project is not a mistake, it's a policy.

THE TENDER NAZI. Nations make policy. People make mistakes.

REBECCA. So where's your remorse? You made a personal mistake, let's see a display of personal remorse, right now.

THE TENDER NAZI. *(quiet)* What do you want me to do? Do you want me to pay reparations? Do you want me to get down on the floor?

REBECCA. Well, what do you think would be appropriate?

THE TENDER NAZI. *(pointed)* Who am I apologizing to, you?

(REBECCA is thrown off.)

REBECCA. Well, I mean, I –

THE TENDER NAZI. You never brutalized anyone?

REBECCA. No.

THE TENDER NAZI. You never surprised yourself by your capacity to destroy another person?

REBECCA. *(intense)* No, I never did. I never did.

THE TENDER NAZI. Then you are very lucky. You can live easily with your mind.

(Pause. **REBECCA** *slumps.)*

REBECCA. *(on the verge of tears again)* I'm so tired. I'm exhausted. I can't do this anymore.

(He moves a few inches closer to her on the bench.)

THE TENDER NAZI. I am sympathetic. Let me comfort you.

REBECCA. *(tired)* No.

THE TENDER NAZI. Please. I would like to.

REBECCA. No. I'm resisting you. I'm horrified by you.

THE TENDER NAZI. *(gently, coaxing)* Really. Come sit by me and let's look at your horror.

(She deliberates a beat, slides slowly towards him along the bench. He takes both of her hands in his and opens them for inspection. The instant they make physical contact a surge passes through **REBECCA.** *She closes her eyes.)*

*(***THE TENDER NAZI** *turns* **REBECCA**'s *hands over and over, examining them precisely)*

THE TENDER NAZI. Hm. Empty.

*(***THE TENDER NAZI** *presses* **REBECCA**'s *hand to the side of his face. He leans into her. She leans into him. They huddle together.)*

(The train slows, the PA makes an unintelligible announcement)

THE TENDER NAZI. Isn't this your stop?

*(***REBECCA** *doesn't open her eyes.)*

REBECCA. Not yet. Not yet.

(Lights shift.)

(The subway roars.)

Scene Twenty-One

(The bedroom. **O** *pacing like a caged animal.* **RAE** *enters.)*

O. Fuck no, I don't have time for this right now.

RAE. All right, I just thought I'd swing by and –

O. *(overlapping)* Look, I'm very busy! I'm waiting for some-one.

RAE. Your friend?

O. Why would a person just leave? And not call?

RAE. *(pointed)* Why indeed?

O. In the middle of a conversation, just walk out the door?

RAE. It's difficult, isn't it, when someone decides that running off into the night is preferable to sitting down and having a reasoned discussion.

(Now **O** *hears her.)*

O. *(dark)* That's *not* what I'm saying.

RAE. I can recall one night I spent *four hours* in the back of a police car, "cruising" the streets of my quiet town looking for someone who made a similar choice. And I thought to myself, "What am *I* doing in the back of a police car? *I've* committed no crime."

O. Not yet, you hadn't.

RAE. Now you see the position I was in.

O. Yes, I imagine hunting down and capturing your own child must have been very stressful for you.

RAE. Extremely. It's horrible, isn't it, imagining what she might be getting into out there. Or who.

O. Stop it. Stop it!

RAE. Then at a certain point you just have to put her out of your mind. You say to yourself that's it, I can't control her, I wash my hands of her. And if her body washes up on the beaches of the sound tomorrow morning, well, what can I do. I tried everything I knew.

O. So, if I follow your playbook here, I should assume that she's dead, in fact drown her in my mind, but if she *does* come home I should trick her into an unmarked car and shackle her and throw her into a dungeon –

RAE. *(indignant)* Dungeon!

O. *(continuous)* – and whack her into next week with narcotizing meds until her mind and her body and her spirit are broken, then I'll have her back, right? Then she'll be mine?

RAE. *(nitpicky)* I'm sorry, I won't stand for "dungeon," that place was the premiere facility of its kind and we were lucky to be able to get you in when –

O. You locked me up like an animal!

RAE. *(overlapping)* You were a danger to yourself and others!

O. I was a child!

RAE. *(furious now)* That's right, you were a frightening, dangerous child. It was like living with a *terrorist*, darling, from your earliest days you were hell-bent on destroying yourself and everything around you, how were we supposed to handle that? I know it has never once occurred to you to imagine what life with you was like for us but you put us in the most untenable positions, over and over again, day after day.

O. I just wanted you to let me go.

RAE. Parents can't just let their children go. They have a responsibility to protect them, even from themselves, even when they don't want that protection.

O. But I didn't –

RAE. *(cutting her off)* I know you live a very comfortable life now where you're responsible for no one and nothing is ever asked of you so you don't understand what it's like to make that kind of decision. With everyone watching you, everyone judging. What choice did we have? What choice did we have? We put everything we had into saving you.

O. *(simply)* You hated me.

RAE. *(very angry)* I did not *hate* you, darling!

O. You wished I was dead.

RAE. I did not wish you were dead!

O. *(overlapping)* You wished I had never been born.

RAE. I wished you had been born completely different.

(O nods, sighs, almost relieved.)

O. *(calm)* I think you'll find that's exactly the same thing.

(Across the room, in the trash can, REBECCA's cell phone begins to ring.)

I have to take this. It might be important.

(RAE makes a move towards O.)

RAE. Darling, I didn't mean that you –

(O shrugs out of reach.)

O. *(calm)* No no, it's okay. We're done.

RAE. Please –

O. From now on as far as you're concerned I *am* dead. Or no, you are. We both are. Whatever. Goodbye.

(O scoops the ringing cell phone up out of the trash.)

(RAE watches as O beeps on the phone. REBECCA does, too.)

(into the phone, receptionist voice)

Hello? No I'm sorry she's not home right now, this is her lover O, may I help you? Yeah, she's been staying out later and later these days, why don't I take a message and have her call you back. It's her mom, right? Hi, yeah, I thought it was you. I mean, we usually fuck right when she gets home in the evenings, but I could have her call you after we're done, say 11:30, 11:45? How late is too late for you?

(beat)

Hello?

(RAE/REBECCA vanishes. O beeps off the phone, carefully returns it to the trash can, crosses deliberately to the bed and sits down on the end of it to wait. Lights shift.)

Scene Twenty-Two

(An Irish sports bar. **REBECCA** *on a cracked, wobbly bar-stool, drinking.* **THE ALL-AMERICAN NAZI** *approaches with frank but well-manicured desire. He's very Street: charcoal pinstripes and jewel-toned French blue Oxford and loosened, grown-up tie. Wet-slick black curly hair. He considers* **REBECCA,** *who doesn't acknowledge him although she's acutely aware of his presence, for a long moment.)*

THE ALL-AMERICAN NAZI. *(finally)* Okay, I'm sorry, you leave me no choice: "What's a nice girl like you doing in a place like this?"

REBECCA. What makes you think that I'm a nice girl?

THE ALL-AMERICAN NAZI. *(thrilled)* Absolutely nothing. I take it back.

REBECCA. No, you're right. I am a nice girl. I just wanted to know what tipped you off.

THE ALL-AMERICAN NAZI. *(thoroughly encouraged)* The shy smile.

(He leans in.)

The beautiful soft brown eyes.

*(**REBECCA** puts her hand up.)*

REBECCA. Yeah, okay.

(indicating her glass)

Why don't you buy me another one of these.

THE ALL-AMERICAN NAZI. I had every intention of doing that. That was – how did you know that was gonna be my next move?

REBECCA. "Next move"? What is this, chess?

THE ALL-AMERICAN NAZI. *(laughing)* Man, you are hard. You are really hard.

*(**REBECCA** doesn't laugh.)*

Do you want me to buy you another drink or not?

REBECCA. No. I take it back. Why don't you give me a cigarette instead?

THE ALL-AMERICAN NAZI. Oh man, I don't have – you want me to –

REBECCA. You are just full of disappointments tonight.

THE ALL-AMERICAN NAZI. Hey, I mean –

REBECCA. Relax. I don't smoke. Have a seat.

> (**THE ALL-AMERICAN NAZI** *leans against the barstool next to* **REBECCA** *'s.*)

> Here's what let's do. You tell me the story of your life, but keep it short. Then I'll tell you the story of my life, but it'll be mostly lies. Then we can go back to your place – you live around here, right?

THE ALL-AMERICAN NAZI. Around *here*? I don't think so. Upper West Side.

REBECCA. Oh, fuck, fuck, fuck. There is no way I'm going all the way back into Manhattan tonight.

THE ALL-AMERICAN NAZI. Well where do *you* live?

REBECCA. Three blocks from here with my very mean, very mentally unstable girlfriend.

THE ALL-AMERICAN NAZI. Girlfriend like…

REBECCA. *(innocent)* Like…?

THE ALL-AMERICAN NAZI. *(prompting)* Like…

REBECCA. Girlfriend like no, we're not going to my place. What's your name, "Craig," probably?

THE ALL-AMERICAN NAZI. No.

REBECCA. "Greg"? Something with a "g" at the end of it.

THE ALL-AMERICAN NAZI. Doug. How did you know?

REBECCA. *(trying it out)* "Doug." "Doug." Are you now or have you ever been a member of a fascist organization, "Doug"?

THE ALL-AMERICAN NAZI. Um, what?

REBECCA. Skinheads, Aryan Nation, Ku Klux Klan? It's okay, you can tell me.

> (**THE ALL-AMERICAN NAZI** *shifts uncomfortably.*)

THE ALL-AMERICAN NAZI. Of course not. I'm – why do you ask?

REBECCA. You're what? You were gonna say "I'm" something. What are you?

THE ALL-AMERICAN NAZI. I was gonna say I'm half-Jewish. My father's Jewish.

REBECCA. But that means nothing. Self-hating Jews were some of the worst collaborators in Nazi-occupied countries.

THE ALL-AMERICAN NAZI. Why are we talking about Nazis all of a sudden?

REBECCA. Because they're everywhere, "Doug." I can't seem to escape them. The cab driver I had this morning was a Nazi. My hairstylist, Andrei, turned out to be a Nazi. My boss at work is a Nazi. Closet case, very cagey. Now you.

THE ALL-AMERICAN NAZI. Look, I don't know what you're talking about. I am not a Nazi. I'm a futures trader. I grew up in Nyack.

REBECCA. *(thoughtfully)* Deep cover. Deep, deep cover.

THE ALL-AMERICAN NAZI. I think maybe I'd better leave you to your…

(gestures vaguely)

…thing.

(THE ALL-AMERICAN NAZI *makes to go.)*

REBECCA. *(restraining him)* No no no, wait. Wait. Sit. Stay.

(He sits back down.)

We both know that we *have* something here, "Doug," I mean, it's just a waste of time to deny it, and it would be nice to think that we're beyond the obligatory flirtatious anecdote exchange, I mean, I'm sure you'd like to dispense with all the preamble, wouldn't you?

THE ALL-AMERICAN NAZI. *(tentative)* Uh, sure.

REBECCA. Sure you would, but that can never happen. You come over here and you want to sleep with me, all your sweet talk is vectoring its way right up my skirt, and I see that, I understand what it's for, but I can't just outright *acknowledge* what's happening or I'll blow my chances with you all to hell, am I right?

THE ALL-AMERICAN NAZI. I guess…

REBECCA. Of course, because that's what honesty does. It tears the social fabric apart.

(*gulps her drink*)

You know, and it's funny that you should mention all this, because I've been thinking a lot about honesty lately, and do you know what I've determined?

THE ALL-AMERICAN NAZI. What's that?

REBECCA. (*delivers it as a maxim*) Honesty is brutality.

THE ALL-AMERICAN NAZI. Huh. You think?

REBECCA. Totally. Think about it. When do you hear people talk about honesty? It's always right before they're about to savage someone else, right?

THE ALL-AMERICAN NAZI. (*thoughtful*) I don't know. Maybe.

REBECCA. No, totally. Someone goes, "Oh, she looks like a whale in that dress, I wouldn't want her to go out like that, and honesty is the best policy, I'm gonna go tell her." Right? Or some girl is like, "Oh no, it's so awful, I cheated on my boyfriend with this guy from the office, it'll kill him if I tell him but honesty is the best policy," and so she tells her boyfriend and she ruins his life, his self-esteem tanks, he can never trust again, the relationship explodes into insults and ashes – who's better off? Who's *happier* now?

THE ALL-AMERICAN NAZI. I guess I see your point.

REBECCA. Yeah, great choice, honesty. Really nice choice.

(*She drinks deeply.*)

THE ALL-AMERICAN NAZI. So…what are you saying?

REBECCA. Just that honesty is *not* my policy. I don't like to cause pain in other people.

THE ALL-AMERICAN NAZI. Because you're a nice girl.

REBECCA. I am.

(beat)

I am.

(She has a moment of vulnerability into her drink. He moves in subtly.)

THE ALL-AMERICAN NAZI. I don't know. I don't think a nice girl would even consider going home with a Nazi from Nyack.

*(**REBECCA** smiles ruefully.)*

REBECCA. Oh, "Doug." How sweet. How naïve you are. Don't you know *only* nice girls fall for Nazis?

(Beat. He smiles down on her.)

THE ALL-AMERICAN NAZI. Why don't we get out of here.

*(He helps **REBECCA** off her barstool, into her coat.)*

REBECCA. There's something I need to tell you before we go, in the interest of total honesty.

THE ALL-AMERICAN NAZI. Shoot.

REBECCA. I'm never going to sleep with you. I'm a lesbian.

*(**REBECCA** puts her hand flat on **THE ALL-AMERICAN NAZI**'s chest as if she's going to push him away, then gathers up a fistful of his shirt and pulls him towards her, kisses him full and slow on the mouth. She releases him. **THE ALL-AMERICAN NAZI** grins, slides his hand around to the small of her back.)*

THE ALL-AMERICAN NAZI. Okay.

(He guides her out of the bar. Lights shift.)

Scene Twenty-Three

*(Twilight, next day. **REBECCA** and **O** in the bedroom.)*

O. I won't ask you where you were.

*(**REBECCA** ignores her. Exquisitely focused, she gathers her things.)*

Are you going to tell me where you were?

(no response)

I was very worried about you.

*(**REBECCA** scoops the cell phone out of the trash can, holds it up for **O** to see.)*

REBECCA. Somehow I don't think that you were.

*(**O** moves towards **REBECCA**. **REBECCA** beeps on the phone, holds it up to her ear.)*

O. I'm sorry –

REBECCA. Guess it's working again. Great.

*(**REBECCA** snaps the phone shut.)*

O. I –

REBECCA. No.

*(**O** reaches for her – **REBECCA** won't be touched.)*

O. Please, just let me –

REBECCA. *No.*

*(**REBECCA** rummages around in the junk under the bed.)*

Where's my suitcase? Where's the suitcase I put right here when I moved in?

O. It's lost.

REBECCA. How do you lose a suitcase in a one-room apartment?

O. *(miserable)* You put it out by the curb on trash day.

REBECCA. *(steely)* I see.

*(**REBECCA** crosses into the bathroom.)*

O. *(low)* Where are you gonna go?

> *(no response)*

You're gonna go stay with your mother, aren't you.

> *(No response. **REBECCA** re-enters with toiletries.)*

You're killing me.

REBECCA. Don't be melodramatic.

> *(O gets down on the floor, crawls to **REBECCA**, curls herself at **REBECCA**'s feet, clutching on to her ankles.)*

What are you – Oh my god.

O. Look at what I'll do for you. I'm on the floor. I'm prostrate before you.

REBECCA. O…

O. Don't go. I shouldn't have done it, I fucked up. I'm sorry. Keep me. Keep me. Please.

> *(**REBECCA** tries to shake O off, can't. She tries to walk to the door, can't because O is clamped to her feet. Drags O klutzily across the floor a little bit. It's awful and funny.)*

REBECCA. You're really gonna regret this part later when you get back in touch with your dignity. You're gonna wish you had stood by the door and waved to me like a flight attendant.

O. *(muffled, miserable, into the floor)* I'm not a flight attendant. I'm a dying girl.

> *(**REBECCA** reaches down to disengage O.)*

REBECCA. Okay, Spook. You're not dying. Come on. It's time.

> *(**REBECCA** strokes O's head.)*

Let go, now, honey. Let go, my love.

> *(**REBECCA** gently loosens O's grip on her ankles, leaves through the stage right door. O remains on the floor in a wrenched heap.)*

> *(Night falls over Queens, over O on the floor.)*

(moonrise)

(distant sirens)

(A subway train passes, subdued: ka-chunk, ka-chunk, ka-chunk.)

(O sleeps in the position **REBECCA** *left her in.)*

Scene Twenty-Four

*(In the darkened apartment, a lamp flips on offstage. A wedge of drinking-glass yellow light falls through the stage right door into the bedroom. **O** lifts her head.)*

(From off, the sound of water running, pots and pans being stacked.)

O. *(still on the floor, calling off)* Spookie?

*(The running water cuts out. **O** sits up.)*

(desperate, hoarse) Spook?

*(**LILY** appears in the stage right doorway, backlit by the hallway light. She shakes water off her hands, wipes her hands on the back of her skirt.)*

LILY. You don't have an apron in there. You don't have a dishrag. You don't even have a paper towel.

*(**LILY** is plump and sweet and slightly tacky. **O** peers at her.)*

Lily Hirschorn. We spoke on the phone…?

(recognition)

O. Are you here for the rest of her stuff?

LILY. No.

O. Did she send you to check up on me?

LILY. I haven't seen her. I don't know where she is.

O. How did you get in?

LILY. I come and I go…

O. *(getting it)* Uh-hunh.

*(**O** lets herself back down onto the floor.)*

LILY. How long have you been on the floor like that?

(no response)

It's not so good for your back.

(no response)

If you need to lie down, why don't you let me make the bed up nice for you –

O. *(a wild, childish cry)* No! From now on I only sleep on hard, flat surfaces!

LILY. Okay, okay. It was a suggestion.

(LILY sits on the bed in the RAE position. She assesses O with some tenderness.)

Boy was I surprised to hear *your* voice on the other end of the line the other night. I was not expecting *that* one. *That* was a shocker. Partly I'm lying, of course. What was I, born yesterday? I can pick up clues when they're dropped. Children always think their mothers have the IQ of a four-year-old, but I've been a few places. I've met a few people. I know the special words for things.

(O lifts her head.)

O. If you're so smart, why didn't you just *tell* her you knew?

LILY. Who, me? I don't tell *that* one anything. I'm not the boss of her.

(LILY gets up, peruses the place.)

I like what you're doing with the contact paper in here. You got a concept going, I like it. You know, I have a few rolls you might want, leftovers from my kitchen re-do, in my basement somewhere. I could dig them out.

O. I'm done with this place.

LILY. Done? You're barely started, it's a wreck in here. You know where you need to get something going is over here, now this is your problem area. Look at these stains.

O. *(dully)* This place is a tomb.

LILY. That's crazy, it's got a ton of potential. A little primer, a little faux work here and there. Hey, I got a coupon for Lowe's, twenty-five percent off, that's something you could use. It's in my purse.

(LILY makes to go into the kitchen after her purse.)

O. I don't want it.

LILY. You don't go to Lowe's?

O. I said I'm *done* with this place.

(O *clutches herself, turns away, trembling.*)

LILY. You don't look so good.

O. (*shivering*) I'm freezing cold.

(LILY *goes to take her cardigan off.*)

LILY. If you're chilly, why don't you take my –

O. No.

LILY. Well then, why don't you let me pour you a nice, hot bath, and you can put those things you've got on in the wash –

(LILY *reaches for* O, O *dodges her.*)

O. No, I can't – I can't take them off! They still smell like her.

(O *moves downstage like a feral child. She crouches on the floor and hugs herself. She brings a fistful of A-shirt to her face and cries into it.*)

LILY. I know you can't hear me when I say this to you, but you're not gonna die.

O. (*muffled, into her knees*) I'm gonna *die.*

LILY. Okay, maybe. But not tonight.

(LILY *sighs.*)

She was always just a little bit out of my reach. This look she would give me, like through a screen door: "I'm right here, just on the other side of this thing." Used to drive me crazy when she was small. You hold a child in your arms, you expect them to look at you with wide-open eyes. I always knew more than half of her was closed to me in there, no matter how hard I stared and stared.

(*beat*)

For you it was fresh. I'm used to it now. What can you do? You love her anyway.

(A beat. O wipes her nose with her A-shirt, crawls over to the bed, rummages underneath it and produces the photo album.)

LILY. *(cont.)* What's this?

(Without touching LILY, O opens the album onto the bed. LILY peers into it.)

Ah…

(O begins to page through the album, narrating as she turns the pages.)

O. *(quiet)* Here she is washing out the Brita filter.

(flips a page of the album)

Here's her making mac and cheese.

(flips another page)

This is her putting the junk mail in the recycling bin.

(flips another page)

Getting her socks on.

(flips another page)

Flossing.

(flips another page)

Sleeping.

(Slowly, O closes the book.)

I miss her very much.

LILY. My baby. I know.

(Lights fade on O and LILY.)

End of Play

OTHER TITLES AVAILABLE FROM SAMUEL FRENCH

SCAB

Sheila Callaghan

Dramtic Comedy / 1-2m, 3f / Simple Set

Anima's sphere of desperation and self-destruction is invaded by the arrival of her perky new roommate, Christa. Moved by a particularly malevolent statue of the Virgin Mary and a houseplant named Susan, Anima and Christa soon enter into a profound and intimate friendship that incurs traumatic results.

"Brilliantly and poetically rendered…[Callaghan's] playful sense of language and her attunement to her characters are enthralling."
– *Time Out Chicago*

"Scab…is a textbook example of promising work, written with a yen for interesting language and liberally salted with well-observed details of the lives of newly minted adults…the play shines."
– *The New York Times*

"Darkly funny forays into the surreal…Callaghan shows talent in the inventive fantasy sequences…A stylish production."
– *The Village Voice*

OTHER TITLES AVAILABLE FROM SAMUEL FRENCH

BODY AWARENESS

Annie Baker

Dramatic Comedy / 2m, 2f / Interior and Areas

Outer Critics Circle John Gassner Award Nominee

It's "Body Awareness" week on a Vermont college campus and Phyllis, the organizer, and her partner, Joyce, are hosting one of the guest artists in their home, Frank, a painter famous for his female nude portraits. Both his presence in the home and his chosen subject instigate tension from the start. Phyllis is furious at his depictions, but Joyce is actually rather intrigued by the whole thing, even going so far as to contemplate posing for him. As Joyce and Phyllis bicker, Joyce's adult son, who may or may not have Asperger's Syndrome, struggles to express himself physically with heartbreaking results.

"The deepest and richest of the three plays by Annie Baker that make up the Shirley, VT Plays Festival...Editor's Pick!"
– *The Boston Globe*

" An engaging new comedy by a young playwright with a probing, understated voice. [...]Its quiet rewards steal up on you."
– *The New York Times*

"Sexuality's endless capacity to make us miserable is the keynote of Annie Baker's gentle satire, which takes just four actors and 90 minutes to spin an astonishingly complex web of emotions and ideas...*Body Awareness* is a smart, modest work about ordinary, flawed people, grasping for connection, but none of it feels small, thanks to Baker's sharp ear for the deeply painful—and funny—longings squirming under her characters' dialogue. What a beautiful start to a young playwright's theatrical body of work."
– David Cote, *Time Out New York*

SAMUELFRENCH.COM

OTHER TITLES AVAILABLE FROM SAMUEL FRENCH

OEDIPUS AT PALM SPRINGS

A Five Lesbian Brothers play written by
Maureen Angelos, Dominique Dibbell,
Peg Healey and Lisa Kron

Comedic Tragedy / 5f

Irreverent theater group the Five Lesbian Brothers get their greasy prints on a classic. *Oedipus at Palm Springs* follows the dark adventure of two couples on a retreat to the desert resort town. While new parents Fran and Con try desperately to jump-start their sex life, May-December love bunnies Prin and Terri can't keep their hands off each other. What begins as a hilarious, boozey weekend takes a horrific turn after a secret is revealed. Two parts comedy with a shot of tragedy shaken over ice, *Oedipus at Palm Springs* is a brave examination of the messy guts of relationships.

"Along the way to the inevitable dark twist is much lightness and enlightenment to revel in–not just a lot of zingy one-liners about commitment, gay life in America, parenthood, and growing older, but also a real sense of these four women as women, friends, and lovers…It may be the saddest comedy you'll ever see."
– *The Boston Globe*

"Richly funny as it is, *Oedipus at Palm Springs* is also a serious inquiry into the unforeseen extremities of despair that can attend the search for a pure and lasting love."
– Charles Isherwood, *New York Times*

"Sensitive storytelling."
– *New York Magazine*

OTHER TITLES AVAILABLE FROM SAMUEL FRENCH

CROOKED

Katherine Trieschmann

Dramatic Comedy / 3f

Fourteen year-old Laney arrives in Oxford, Mississippi with a twisted back, a mother in crisis and a burning desire to be writer. When she befriends Maribel Purdy, a fervent believer in the power of Jesus Christ to save her from the humiliations of high school, Laney embarks on a hilarious spiritual and sexual journey that challenges her mother's secular worldview and threatens to tear their fragile relationship apart.

"The work of a big accomplished writer's voice…a gem
of a discovery."
– *The New York Times*

"Gorgeous almost beyond belief."
– *The London Times*

"This is a wonderfully neat play, at once simple and complex,
grappling with big issues - matters of faith, fantasy and the flesh -
while keeping its sneakers firmly planted on the suburban topsoil of
adolescent angst and domestic frictions."
– *The Daily Telegraph*

CPSIA information can be obtained at www.ICGtesting.com
Printed in the USA
LVOW06s1954261215

467669LV00088B/2183/P